For my oldest prehistoric friends,
Paul, Rob, Ceri, and Andy – GG

For my wife Angelika xx – DG

Quarto is the authority on a wide range of topics.

Quarto educates, entertains and enriches the lives of
our readers—enthusiasts and lovers of hands-on living.
www.quartoknows.com

Author: Greg Gormley
Illustrator: Dean Gray
Designer: Victoria Kimonidou
Editor: Ellie Brough

This edition first published in 2020 by QED Publishing,
an imprint of The Quarto Group.
The Old Brewery, 6 Blundell Street,
London N7 9BH, United Kingdom.
T (0)20 7700 6700 F (0)20 7700 8066
www.QuartoKnows.com

A catalogue record for this book is available from the British Library.

ISBN 978 0 7112 5066 6

Manufactured in Guangdong, China TT122019

9 8 7 6 5 4 3 2 1

ALL ABOUT
ALLOSAURS

GREG GORMLEY  DEAN GRAY

QED

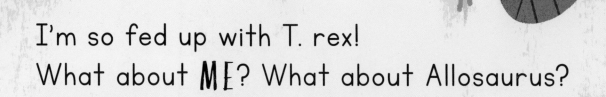

I'm so fed up with T. rex!
What about ME? What about Allosaurus?

Nobody ever wants to know about me.
It's always T. rex this and T. rex that.

She's just a great big show-off.
Well I've had quite enough.

TOP DINO

The best of the dinosaurs (by far!)
would have to be T. rex. She's totally
ROARSOME!

I know, I'll write a book all about myself and then everybody will know how awesome I AM!

"Can I be in it, Allosaurus?"

No, Triceratops, it's all about ME.

"But I'm your top best friend."

Oh, alright then.

"Yay!"

Triceratops is terrifically strong. She has a fabulous collar, three horns on her head and is very good at eating her vegetables.

Now, where to begin about me, hmm...

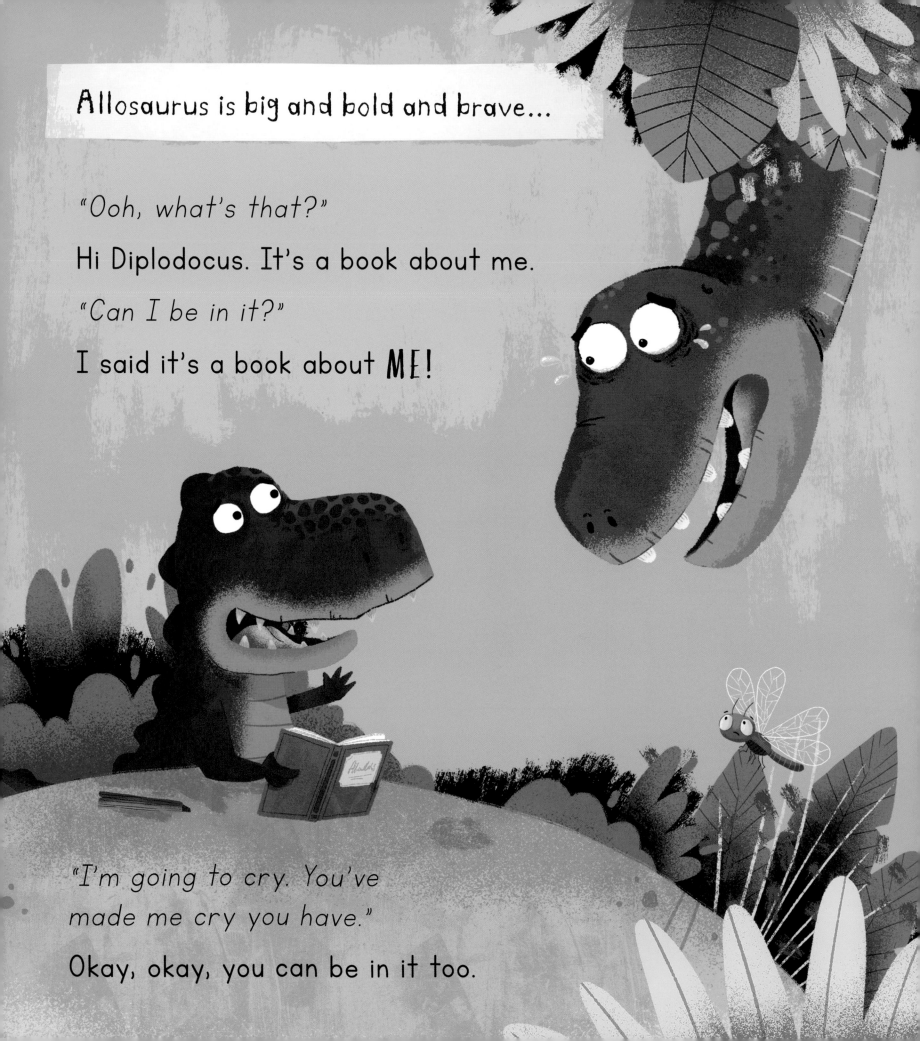

Allosaurus is big and bold and brave...

"Ooh, what's that?"

Hi Diplodocus. It's a book about me.

"Can I be in it?"

I said it's a book about ME!

"I'm going to cry. You've
made me cry you have."

Okay, okay, you can be in it too.

Diplodocus is the longest dinosaur.
He is really, really long with a tiny,
weeny head. He can bash other
dinosaurs with his tail if they are naughty.

*"You could call it
'Diplodocus and I'."*

NO!

Right, maybe I'll get a bit of peace now.

CRASH

Oh no, the Velociraptor twins!

"What are you doing?"

Writing a book.

"Can we be in it, oh go on, can we please, pleeease, pretty prehistoric please?"

YES! Now leave me alone.

Velociraptors are a bit of a nuisance but they are fast, clever and very good at working together. And they have very long, sharp claws – ow!

Back to me, finally.

Allosaurus is an attractive fellow...

"Look out below!"

Pteranodon, what is it?

"T. rex is looking for you and she looks rather grumpy."

Thanks, I owe you one.

"*Maybe you can put me in your book?*"

Oh, for goodness sake, all right.

Pteranodon can fly! Cool or what? He has no teeth in his beak and likes to eat fish for his supper. He has longer wings than any bird!

RO

Erm, T. rex, how are you?

"Cross! You've been mean about me."

Oh?

"Yes, a T. rex has feelings too, you know."

I'm sorry. I'll put a fact file about you right at the beginning of my book. How about that?

"Wonderful! I've always wanted to be in a book, ever since I was an egg."

Well, I've finished my book and the only dinosaur not in it, is ME. I'm nothing special, nobody's interested in me.

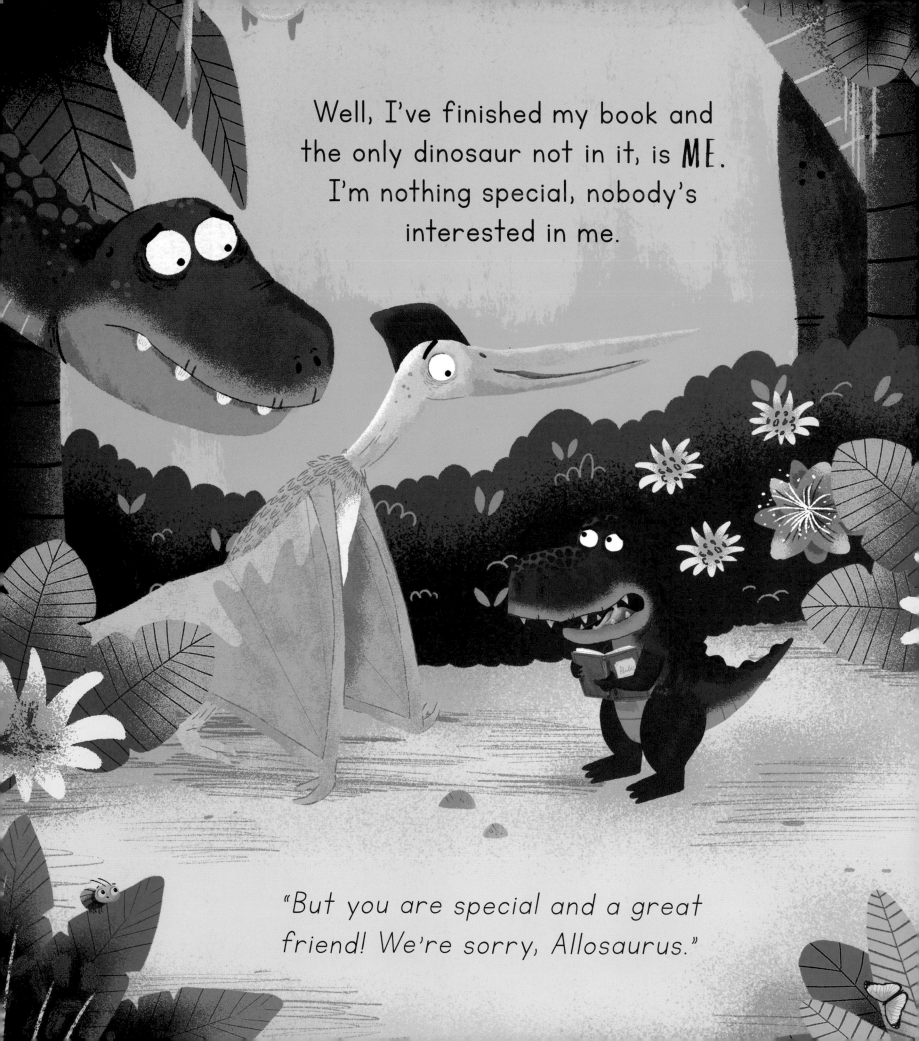

"But you are special and a great friend! We're sorry, Allosaurus."

"We've all been so selfish and you've been so kind. Write it again but just about you this time."

"You could call it...

'ALL ABOUT ALLOSAURUS'."

Thanks! But I'm still going to keep all of you in it. It's much better that way.

"HURRAY!"

And maybe I'll just put a little bit about myself in the back.

NEXT STEPS

Discussion and comprehension

Discuss the story with the children and ask the following questions, encouraging them to take turns and give full answers if they can. Offer support by turning to the appropriate pages of the book if needed.

- Why was Allosaurus fed up with T. rex at the beginning of the story?
- What do you think it means to be 'selfish'? How were the other dinosaurs selfish?
- Who said they were Allosaurus's top best friend?
- How would you feel if you were Allosaurus?
- Everyone was happy in the end but how could this story have ended differently?

Compare two dinosaurs

Give each child a piece of A4 paper with four marked boxes. Put the title 'Compare Two Dinosaurs' and head the bottom two boxes: 'How are they different?' and 'How are they the same?'. Give children print outs of the book and ask them to draw two different dinosaurs from the book in the top two boxes and label them with their names. Using information from the book, ask them to write two or three sentences about the differences and similarities of the dinosaurs that they have chosen in the bottom two boxes. For example: 'they are both fierce' and 'one is big and one is small'.

Make yourself into a dinosaur

Give each child a large piece of brightly coloured sugar paper, a paint brush, some contrasting coloured paints and a thick black felt pen. Ask the children to begin by choosing a paint colour and making a handprint in the middle of the paper. They then need to turn the paper upside down to turn their handprint into a dinosaur. The thumb will be the tail, the fingers make legs and they can paint on a head and neck with a brush. They can add any other features, including claws, with a pen. When they have finished, help them to write their name on the top of the picture with 'osaurus' or 'saurus' at the end. For example, 'Johnosaurus' or 'Katiesaurus'.

Allosaurus Facts

Name means: different lizard

Size: not as big as T. rex

Teeth: not as long or sharp as T. rex's

Mood: much happier

Skill: writes books